BAD BOYZ: LEA

D1149393

Alan Durant has been footb... eight. On the field, he peaked early, playing for two seasons in the Collingwood Boys Junior School football team, scoring one goal! After that, it was all downhill. He supports Manchester United and his favourite player of all time is George Best, after whom he named his one and only goldfish. Sadly, the goldfish died. He has passed his football talents on to his son Kit, who plays in a little league – and around the house with a pair of rolled-up socks. Bad Boyz is based on children he has met during his career as an author and football spectator ... you know who you are!

Alan Durant's football stories have appeared in various anthologies, including two collections of *Gary Lineker's Favourite Football Stories*; *On Me 'Ead, Santa*; and *Football Shorts*. He is also the author of the Leggs United series about a family football team managed by a ghost. The series and Alan himself were featured in a recent Children's Bafta Award-winning BBC TV programme. His other work ranges from picture books for young children to novels and mystery stories for young adults. Alan lives just south of London with his wife, Jinny, and three children, Amy, Kit and Josie. He doesn't expect to get a call from Sven Goran Eriksson.

Books by the same author

Bad Boyz: Kicking Off
K.O. Kings
Barmy Army
Creepe Hall
Return to Creepe Hall
Creepe Hall For Ever!
Jake's Magic
Star Quest: Voyage to the Greylon Galaxy
Spider McDrew
Happy Birthday, Spider McDrew
Little Troll
Little Troll and the Big Present
Leggs United (series)
Football Fun

BAD BOYZ:
LEAGUES APART

ALAN DURANT

To Michael
with best wishes!

30/8/06

WALKER BOOKS
AND SUBSIDIARIES

LONDON · BOSTON · SYDNEY · AUCKLAND

First published 2001 by Walker Books Ltd
87 Vauxhall Walk, London SE11 5HJ

6 8 10 9 7 5

Text © 2001 Alan Durant
Bad Boyz logo © 2001 Phil Schramm
Cover photography by Cliff Birtchell
Cover design by Walker Books Ltd

This book has been typeset in Futura book

Printed in Great Britain by J.H. Haynes & Co. Ltd

All rights reserved. No part of this book may be reproduced,
transmitted or stored in an information retrieval system in
any form or by any means, graphic, electronic or mechanical,
including photocopying, taping and recording, without
prior written permission from the publisher.

British Library Cataloguing in Publication Data:
a catalogue record for this book
is available from the British Library

ISBN 0-7445-5990-1

For Kit, Chris, Jon, Vinnie for their comments – and with a banner wave to all the players, parents, managers, dogs, etc., who turn up for Little League football every Saturday morning

1

"Wow!"

"Cool!"

"Wick-ed!"

The brand-new football shirt, held up by Mr Davies, received the unanimous approval of his team. In their only game so far, Bad Boyz had played in a strip borrowed from their school. Now, for their first match in the Appleton Little League, they were to play in their very own kit. The shirt displayed by the manager even had the team's name emblazoned across it in big black letters: **BAD BOYZ**. It also bore the name of their sponsors: the Doorstep Dairy.

"Max's dad has done us proud," said Mr Davies as he handed round the new shirts. Max's dad was a milkman with the Doorstep

Dairy and he'd managed to persuade his employers to pay for his son's team's strip. The dairy's chairman was a keen football fan and liked to support local ventures.

"We're gonna look like Brazil," said Dareth, the Bad Boyz captain, holding his shirt up in front of his chest. The shirt was a bright custard yellow.

"Yeah!" squeaked Andrew, alias Bloomer, the smallest member of the team. His shirt hung down almost to his knees.

"Hey, look, Bloomer's got his nightie on," laughed Jordan, the team's only girl.

"Just as long as he doesn't go to sleep in the game," said Mr Davies pointedly.

Bloomer was famous for his tiny attention span. It frequently got him into detention at school – where, in the past at least, he had regularly been joined by the rest of the team. It wasn't for nothing that they were called Bad Boyz.

When they were dressed, Mr Davies called them round for a team talk. He glanced around to check they were all there: Dareth, Sadiq, Jordan, Bloomer, Sung-Woo, Kyle...

"Max!" he called. "Where are you?"

Right on cue, Max appeared from the toilet – wearing his dark blue shorts on his head.

"You called, master?" he boomed, as if he were a genie summoned from a magic lamp. The others laughed.

"Max," Mr Davies sighed, "put your shorts on your butt and let's get this show on the road. We've got a match to play."

Max bowed low. "Yes, master," he intoned. He took the shorts off his head, grinning hugely.

Finally, all the team were fully dressed and ready for action.

"Right," said Mr Davies. "This is a big day for us, isn't it?"

"Mmm." There was a general murmur of agreement.

"We've come a long way in the last couple of months," the coach continued. "Now we've reached our goal. We're going to play in the little league. Well, you are anyway. I'll just be watching from the sidelines. I've done my bit; now it's up to you." He paused to glance around the semicircle of children in front of him. His mind returned to that day in early spring when, fed up with seeing the same seven children in detention all the time, he'd suggested the idea of forming them into a football team. Now, here they were, looking every centimetre a team in their new yellow and blue strip...

A loud fart brought these fond thoughts to a sudden end. There were groans of disgust.

"Kyle!" Sadiq accused.

Kyle, the team's goalkeeper, was a picture of wobbly innocence. "Me?" he protested. He frowned so hard, his small eyes almost disappeared into his pale face like raisins into a bowl of semolina. "I didn't do nuffing! It was Sung-Woo."

"I think we'd better get out in the open," said Mr Davies, "before we're all gassed."

His players needed no second invitation. At once, the room echoed with the sound of studs tapping and clumping their way across the wooden floor.

Only Sung-Woo remained. His face, as ever, bore a serious, slightly baffled expression.

"Is no gas," he said gravely. "Is just my bottom. I have too many beans for breakfast.

Beans make you—"

"Yes, thank you, Sung-Woo," Mr Davies interjected. "It's your feet I'm interested in. Now, off you go and get kicking that ball. I want to see some goals from you today." Sung Woo was the team's striker.

"Yes, sir," he said – and he almost smiled.

2

Bad Boyz' first opponents were Vinnie's Vulcans. They were already out on the pitch in their green and white shirts and green shorts. They were practising their shooting when Bad Boyz ran out of the changing room. A small, ginger-haired boy flicked a ball into the air and volleyed a shot past his keeper, high into the back of the net.

"He looks all right," said Dareth appreciatively.

"Nah," said Kyle. "I'd've saved that easy." He stretched out a large meaty arm, miming a save.

"You'd never have got near it, you big ape," said Sadiq. He and Kyle often had a go at each other. In the past at school their arguments had frequently led to blows and, later, detention. Since Bad Boyz had come together though, they'd managed to control themselves – most of the time.

"You don't know nuffing," Kyle retorted hotly.

Mr Davies arrived just in time. "Hey, you're on the same side, you two," he chided. "You'll boost the other team's confidence if they see you arguing among yourselves. Now, let's get warmed-up…"

Warming-up was Bad Boyz' least favourite activity and they always met its announcement with a collective grumble. But Mr Davies insisted on it. Before their twice-weekly training sessions and now before this first match against the Vulcans, they went through a rigorous routine of bends, stretches, jogs, jumps and sprints. Only then did they get to kick a ball around.

They divided in half, forming two straight lines, with the front players, Dareth and Sadiq, facing each other. Mr Davies threw Dareth a ball and the exercise started. Dareth passed the ball to Sadiq then sprinted across to the back of the opposite line. Sadiq trapped the ball and passed to the new front player in the other line, Sung-Woo. Then Sadiq sprinted to the back of the opposite line. And so it went on, until everyone had received and passed the ball at least five times.

After that, they practised shooting. Again they stood in a line. This time the front player was Jordan. She passed to Mr Davies, who was standing midway between her and Kyle in goal. Mr Davies tapped it to his left, while Jordan ran on and shot first time. The ball whizzed wide – much to Kyle's amusement.

"You wanna get some glasses, Jordan," he laughed.

"You want to get a brain, Kyle," Jordan responded.

"Just get the ball, Jordan," said Mr Davies.

Kyle was good at this exercise and very difficult to beat. He wasn't the most agile of keepers, but he made full use of his size to block the shots that were on target. He let in only a couple of goals from the many shots fired at him.

"It's like trying to get past the Incredible Hulk," moaned Sadiq, as Kyle pulled off yet another comfortable save.

"Well, let's hope the Vulcans feel like that

too," said Mr Davies. "I don't want any silly goals going in our end. Let's try to keep a clean sheet. OK, Max?"

"Sir!" Max shouted, raising his hand to his head in a military salute. Then he toppled sideways to the ground.

Mr Davies smiled. Max loved to clown around now, but when the whistle blew for the match to start he'd be the most competitive player on the pitch. It was a transformation that never ceased to amaze all those who knew him.

And just at that moment, the whistle did indeed blow for the captains to go to the centre circle for the toss of the coin. Dareth walked forward for Bad Boyz and the ginger-haired boy for Vinnie's Vulcans. The referee introduced himself, then asked the two captains to shake hands.

"Right, who's going to call?" he asked.

"I will," said the ginger-haired boy quickly. He called "heads". It was.

"We'll have kick-off," he said. "Which end do you want?"

"We'll stay as we are," said Dareth. He grinned. "Our keeper don't like to move much."

The ginger-haired boy looked past Dareth to where Kyle was sitting on his goal line. Then he grinned too. "Don't worry," he said. "All he'll have to do is turn round … to pick the ball out of the net."

Dareth shook his head. "He don't like to do that neither," he said.

The other boy snorted. "Sounds like he doesn't like to do anything."

"Yeah, he does," said Dareth. "He likes to squash ginger nuts."

With that he turned and walked back to take up his place for kick-off.

3

Vinnie's Vulcans had about a dozen supporters. Bad Boyz had one – and that was Mr Davies.

Max's dad had hoped to come, but the dairy was short-staffed and he had to do a second milk round. The other mums and dads were either working or had other commitments on a Saturday morning. Some, like Dareth's, were missing completely.

Mr Davies did his best to make himself heard, but he felt a bit like a tinkly triangle in a band of trombones. The Vulcans manager, Vinnie, was particularly loud. He had a rough, deep voice, which he made full use of – bellowing instructions and criticism between puffs on his cigarette.

"Stuart, get your finger out!"

"I said *run*, Ryan. A snail could do better than that!"

"Oi, what're you two doing back there? Havin' a tea party?"

"Kieron, if I wanted you on the left wing, I'd've put you there! Now get back and defend!"

These shouts were usually echoed by one or more of Vinnie's fellow supporters, which meant there was rarely a quiet moment.

It was pretty hectic on the pitch, too.

It was the first league match for both sides and they played as if it might be their last. The tackling was strong and there was fierce competition for every ball. Sometimes too fierce. After one clash between Sadiq and Ryan, the ginger-haired boy, the referee took them both aside and warned them to cool down.

Vinnie wasn't impressed. "Come on, ref, it's a man's game!" he grunted, waving his cigarette in the air. As it happened, the player closest to him was Jordan. She turned and glared and for a couple of minutes, Vinnie went silent.

"Come on, Bad Boyz!" Mr Davies called,

taking advantage of the sudden lull.

So far, his team had done well, especially as they were playing into the breeze. With five minutes to go in the first half, the score was still 0–0 and there was little to choose between the teams. The Vulcans had had more of the ball, but apart from a couple of good shots from Ryan, they hadn't created any chances. At the other end, Dareth had a shot cleared off the line following a corner. At half-time 0–0 would be a good score, Mr Davies reckoned. But it wasn't to be.

An attack by the Vulcans ended with the ball rolling harmlessly out of play for a goal kick. As Vinnie shouted in disgust at his players, Kyle placed the ball on the line at the edge of his goal area. Glancing round, he saw Bloomer unmarked just outside the penalty box. Quickly, he kicked the ball towards him. However, at that moment, a large plane flew overhead and Bloomer's attention went with it.

"Bloomer!" Kyle shrieked. But by the time Bloomer reacted, Ryan had stepped in and stolen the ball. Sadiq and Max had pushed too far forward and the Vulcan player had a clear run on goal. As Kyle moved out to meet the Vulcan player, Ryan dragged the ball back, flipped it up and, just as he had in practice, volleyed it powerfully into the net. Kyle had no chance.

"YES!" yelled the Vulcans' supporters.

Vinnie was ecstatic. He took a last deep drag on his cigarette then tossed the stub to the ground, as if he were casting away all his cares.

"That's the way, Vulcans!" he exhorted. "Now, let's get another!"

"Never mind, Bad Boyz. Heads up!" Mr Davies called. But his voice was lost amid the loud celebrations around him.

4

At half-time, the score was still 1–0, though Ryan had come close to putting the Vulcans further in the lead. This time his shot had hit the post and Max had cleared the rebound.

"Told you you wouldn't save his shot, didn't I?" Sadiq grumbled to Kyle as the team gathered gloomily for their oranges.

"It weren't my fault," said Kyle. "It was Bloomer, weren't it? He weren't lookin'."

"Yeah, well, you still didn't save the shot, did you?" Sadiq persisted.

"Barthez wouldn't've saved that shot," Dareth pointed out.

"That's right," Mr Davies agreed. "Kyle's doing fine – and so are you all. There's no need to be despondent. We can still win this one, especially now we've got the wind behind us. They've only got one really good player, but he's getting too much space. Max, I want you to mark him, OK? Everywhere he goes, you go too. If we can stop that Ryan playing, then they'll struggle."

The peep of the referee's whistle summoning the teams for the second half was followed by a deafening roar from Vinnie.

"Here we go, Vulcans!" he rasped. "Hundred miles an hour!"

"I wish someone could stop *him*," Jordan complained, putting her hands over her ears.

"A couple of goals should do it," said Mr Davies. He smiled at his striker. "Eh, Sung-Woo?"

Sung-Woo frowned. "I try," he said. Then he farted. "Sorry," he apologized as the others quickly moved away to take up their places on the pitch.

"Well, you've certainly got the wind behind *you*, Sung-Woo," Mr Davies remarked, before retreating to the touch-line.

The second half began as competitively as the first. Jordan made a couple of tackles that had Vinnie roaring with outrage, though the referee saw nothing wrong. He did blow his whistle for a foul, though, when one of the Vulcans tripped Dareth. "You gotta be joking, ref!" Vinnie howled.

The referee ignored him.

Mr Davies called his players forward. "Let's have a big kick into the area, Sadiq," he urged.

Sadiq did as his coach instructed. He booted the ball towards the Vulcans goal. It was a strong kick but the wind made it even stronger. The ball soared into the air and only started to drop when it had gone over the heads of the players gathered in the penalty box. The Vulcans keeper dived to his left, but couldn't reach the ball which, to everyone's surprise, bounced against the post and into the net. Bad Boyz had equalized.

"Yes!" Now it was Mr Davies's turn to celebrate. Vinnie, meanwhile, put his head in his hands.

"I – you – er," he spluttered, before lapsing into rare silence.

Sadiq's team-mates ran to congratulate him. For once, he was happy. He didn't lose his smile even when Kyle shouted to him that the goal was a fluke.

"Who cares?" he shrugged – and no one argued.

For a while, the game was close, with neither side making any clear chances. But the Vulcans were tiring. They were starting to have difficulty getting out of their half. When they did, Max and Sadiq were waiting for them. Max was superb. He followed Ryan like a lanky Rottweiler, stepping in to make a tackle whenever the Vulcan striker got the ball. As a result, Ryan lost heart and drifted out of the game – much to his manager's annoyance.

"Pull your finger out, Ryan, or I'll drop you next week!" Vinnie bullied, but his words only made Ryan more dejected. Mr Davies felt sorry for the boy. In the end, though, it wasn't the Bad Boyz coach or a Vulcan team-mate who stood up for Ryan; it was Sadiq.

"Why don't you shut up?" he yelled at Vinnie finally, after the Vulcans manager had bellowed yet another threat at his star player.

Vinnie nearly swallowed his cigarette. He looked as if he might explode.

"Oi, you little toe-rag!" he exclaimed at last, when he'd stopped coughing.

Mr Davies was about to say something

when the referee intervened.

"Right, that's enough!" he warned the Vulcans manager. "Anymore outbursts like that and I'll stop the match."

"Come on, ref!" Vinnie protested. But now even his fellow supporters turned on him and told him to give it a rest. This was too much for Vinnie. He threw up his hands with an angry "humph" and walked away.

Later, he was probably glad he did, because he wouldn't have liked what followed one bit: Bad Boyz scored with their very next attack. Jordan and Dareth played a neat one-two, then the captain beat the last defender and walloped the ball into the net.

For the last ten minutes, it was virtually one-way traffic. Sung-Woo went close, Dareth hit the bar, Jordan hit a post. Then Bloomer went on a scampering run down the left, leaving two opponents in his wake before crossing the ball to Sung-Woo. His shot was straight at the keeper, but the ball rebounded to Dareth, who smashed in his second goal. Ryan, who'd perked up again since his manager had departed, did pull a goal back minutes later, but the Vulcans were a beaten team.

There was still time for one more goal though and, from where Mr Davies was standing, a bizarre goal it was. Dareth took a corner on the right. The ball arrived in the centre of the goal – and suddenly everyone turned away from it, holding their noses. Well, everyone except Sung-Woo, who sidefooted the ball into the corner of the net.

Soon after, the referee blew his whistle for the end of the game. Bad Boyz had won their first game in the Appleton Little League, four goals to two.

5

The Appleton Little League had a magazine. It was called *Top Shots* and contained news, results and match reports from the league. Mr Davies brought in a copy to show his players in the week after their second match – against Dorking Runners. Jordan read it out to the others.

Appleton Little League

Bad Boyz *vs* Dorking Runners

Match Report by Stan Reynolds,
League Secretary

THE SECOND WEEK of the league threw up some interesting fixtures. Among them was the clash between Bad Boyz and Dorking Runners. Both teams had got off to a winning start and this promised to be a close game. It was a drizzly morning, but thanks to the efforts of Mr Gutteridge the pitch was in excellent condition. (Well done, Reg!)

The match started slowly. Both teams looked as if they wished they were still snugly tucked-up in their beds and some of the spectators felt the same way! Luckily, Mrs Gutteridge was on hand with cups of steaming hot coffee. Meanwhile, on the pitch, Bad Boyz were awarded a penalty when their captain, Gareth Clements, was tripped in the Dorking penalty box. He took the penalty himself to give Bad Boyz the lead. But Dorking Runners were back level only minutes later when they scored from their first real chance of the game. The scorer was Danny Stewart. Soon after this, the referee, Simon Burnside, had to have a stern word with one of the Bad Boyz players, Sadiq Ali, for constantly arguing with his decisions. The referees put in a lot of good work and should not have to put up with this kind of behaviour.

The pressure was on Bad Boyz now and Dorking Runners went ahead with a run and shot from Danny Stewart. The Bad Boyz keeper got his hand to the shot but could not keep it out. It was a good effort but he spoiled it by throwing a big clump of muddy grass at his opponent's back as he turned away to celebrate. The referee had to have another stern word. The game continued quietly until half-time, except for a brief pause when a small terrier ran across the pitch and did a mess in the centre circle. Spectators really must keep their dogs under control. Luckily, Mr Gutteridge was at hand with his shovel and bucket to remove the offending pile.

Having eaten one of Mrs Gutteridge's excellent pies, I returned, as did the players, fully refreshed for the second half. Bad Boyz soon scored an equalizer through their striker,

Woo-Song. The same player scored again minutes later and so did Gareth Clements. Andrew "Bloomer" Dean completed the scoring with a rather lucky deflection off a defender. The final score was Bad Boyz 5, Dorking Runners 2.

Well played, both teams, and well done to Mr and Mrs Gutteridge!

"Is that it?" Max scoffed. "That was pants."

"Lucky deflection?" squeaked Bloomer. "That was a brilliant goal."

"And that bloke got our names wrong," Dareth complained. "Gareth and Woo-Song!"

"Kyle could've written a better report than that," Sadiq remarked.

"My gran's budgie could've written a better report than that," said Dareth.

"That bloke don't know what he's talking about," Kyle grumbled. "All that stuff about me chucking mud. I never did nuffing. I was just clearing the goalmouth, that's all. It weren't my fault if the striker was walking in front of me."

"All he was interested in was his pie," said Jordan.

"Who ate all the pies, who ate all the pies," Max sang. "You fat b—"

Mr Davies raised his hand. "All right, Max, enough," he ordered. He stared hard at his team. "Now look, you lot, if you think you can do better, why don't you?"

"Eh?" said Sadiq.

"What do you mean?" Jordan queried.

"I mean that you should produce your *own* match report," Mr Davies continued. "Take it in turns to write it maybe. You could use one of the computers in the ITC suite." He nodded at Jordan. "You're an artist, Jordan. You could design a heading and some graphics. We could put the report up on the school notice-board – and send a copy to the league, too." He smiled. "Show them how it should be done."

Jordan shrugged. "OK," she said, as if she didn't really care one way or the other. "But I don't want anyone else interfering."

"We could put in the results and league tables too," Dareth suggested.

Jordan scowled. "I'm not doing that," she said. "That's numbers and stuff."

For the first time, Sung-Woo spoke. "I do that," he said simply.

31

"Yeah, Sung-Woo's wicked at maths and he's brilliant on the computer and all," Max enthused. Sung-Woo smiled modestly. "He helps me with my maths homework sometimes and I help him with his English." Sung-Woo nodded. Max contorted his face ridiculously. "How now brown cow?" he pronounced comically.

"Very useful," said Mr Davies, "if you need to have a conversation with a cow."

"Well, his dad *is* a milkman," Dareth pointed out.

"Ah, yes, that reminds me," said Mr Davies. "We should send a copy of the match reports to the dairy too. You'd better put their name at the top, Jordan: Bad Boyz sponsored by the Doorstep Dairy."

"I'm not drawing any cows, though," Jordan declared.

"Sir!" Bloomer squawked urgently.

"Yes, Bloomer," said Mr Davies. "What is it?"

Bloomer frowned. "I've forgotten," he said.

6

The first official Bad Boyz report appeared nearly a fortnight later. It would have been sooner, only Bloomer deleted the computer file by mistake and the report had to be typed in all over again. Luckily, only the text was lost, not Jordan's artwork, or Bloomer would have been in serious trouble. Jordan said she'd have ripped out his guts and fed them to the caretaker's dog.

The author of the first report was Max. But Max being Max, he couldn't just *write* the report, he had to make it sound as if he was actually commentating on the game.

BAD BOYZ
SPONSORED BY THE DOORSTEP DAIRY
Bad Boyz *vs* Dart United
Match Report
by "Mad" Max Driscoll

Hi, folks!

This is Mad Max reporting on the top Appleton Little League clash between the fabulous Bad Boyz and their opponents, Fart United. Sorry, I mean Dart United. Bad Boyz kick off and go on the attack. Sung-Woo taps the ball to Dareth. He kicks the ball back to Sadiq, who boots it out to Bloomer. He passes the ball back to Dareth. He goes past one player, then another. He shoots! He misses! Only joking. He scores! Bad Boyz take the lead in the first minute. *Ama*-zing! The crowd go wild. "One Dareth Clements, there's only one Dareth Clements!" they sing. Oh no, that's not the crowd singing, it's Dareth!

Dart United don't know what's hit them. Bad Boyz are all over them. Sadiq and

Max are having a blinder. They're unbeatable. And behind them there's Kyle: Mount Everest in goalie gloves.

Now Jordan's got the ball. She runs at the Dart United defence. She crosses the ball to Sung-Woo. He goes past the last defender as if he wasn't there. He shoots. He scores! 2–0! What a goal! Is that a smile on Sung-Woo's face? Yes, I do believe it is. Sung-Woo has smiled, ladies and gentlemen. How about that?

It's all Bad Boyz now. Dart United may as well go home, 'cos Dareth's just knocked in a third. 3–0 at half-time! Who'd have thought it? These Bad Boyz are out of this world. Look at them suck those oranges. They're on fire!

The second half is like the first half – only it comes after it. Bad Boyz attack like demons. Jordan scores, then Sung-Woo scores, then Dareth scores. Kyle makes a good save. Bloomer spots a helicopter. Sadiq goes on a run and wins a corner. Is there no end to the excitement, folks? No. Well, not for Max anyway, 'cos when the corner comes over, he leaps like a wombat and heads the ball into the net. It's the goal of the match! It's the goal of the season! Is there no end to this boy's talent? To find out, you'll just have to read next week's Bad Boyz match report.

This is "Mad" Max Driscoll saying, "Goodbye and good riddance!"

7

Mr Davies was very pleased with the report. As he pointed out to the less enthusiastic head-teacher, Mr Fisher (alias Piranha), in making the reports his players had to use computer, writing, number and design skills – and it kept them out of trouble.

"Yes, I suppose you're right," Piranha replied. "But lavatories aren't on the school curriculum, so please ask your players to cut the toilet humour. I really don't want that sort of language on my notice-board."

Mr Davies passed on this instruction to his team.

"It was only a joke," Max protested.

"I know," said Mr Davies. "But in future, no farts. Understand?"

"OK," said Max.

At once, as if on cue, a loud thunderclap ripped through the air.

"Sorry," said Sung-Woo with a huge grin.

Mr Davies sighed and beat a hasty retreat.

Another reason he was pleased with the reports was that compiling them, he believed, was good for teamwork – a quality on which he laid great importance.

At the team training sessions, the team often did exercises designed to encourage them to work together, as well as improving their football skills. One of their favourites was an exercise in which they split into two teams and took it in turns to dribble through a set of cones – without touching them – before lifting the ball and keeping it in the air for five kicks. Then they had to sprint back with the ball and pass it to the next member of their team.

Mr Davies kept a close watch on them to make sure they did each part of the exercise properly before they moved on to the next. Because the teams were uneven, the first to go in the team with three players went again at the end to make it fair. It was very competitive, but usually undertaken in good spirit with lots of applause and appreciation for feats of skill – and the odd howl of derision when someone made a complete mess of things.

The team's football skills had improved hugely in the two months they'd been playing together. Even the less gifted players, like Kyle and Sadiq, carried out the training exercises quite capably. As a unit, the team was functioning well – on and off the field.

The results continued to be impressive – as the match reports recorded. Sadiq and Kyle each wrote a report with help from Mr Davies, who also took out some of the more dodgy comments – such as Sadiq's reference to one referee as "a cow pat on legs" or Kyle calling an opposition striker "a fat turd".

Below each report was the current league table, carefully updated by Sung-Woo, who was given the complete set of results every Monday morning by Mr Davies. This is how the table stood after the first five weeks:

"You're doing really well with those tables, Sung-Woo. Keep it up," Mr Davies enthused.

"It's easy," said Sung-Woo. "I show you if you like."

"Why don't you show us all?" Mr Davies suggested.

Sung-Woo shook his head. "They say they're no interested in numbers."

"I bet they all know how many goals they've scored, though," said Mr Davies.

Teams	Played	Wo
Bad Boyz	5	5
Terminators	5	3
Vinnie's Vulcans	5	3
Hornets	5	2
Dorking Runners	5	2
Eddy's Eagles	5	1
X Club 7	5	0
Dart United	5	0

A small smile dimpled Sung-Woo's cheeks. "But Kyle doesn't want to know how many he's let in," he remarked.

"No," Mr Davies agreed. "I bet he doesn't."

With five weeks gone and Bad Boyz top of the table, everything was going as smooth as syrup. Nothing, it seemed, could go wrong.

But with Bad Boyz, trouble was never far away…

Drawn	Lost	For	Against	Points
0	0	25	7	15
1	1	21	5	10
1	1	18	8	10
3	0	18	7	9
2	1	11	11	8
1	3	11	13	4
0	5	2	22	0
0	5	1	34	0

8

The bubble burst the very next game: Bad Boyz were beaten 2–1 by one of their main rivals, Hornets. It was the first ever defeat they had suffered and they were as sick as the sickest parrot.

After the match, Mr Davies tried to lift his team. They were unlucky to lose, he said, but he was sure that the defeat would make them even stronger and more determined.

But then came the match report.

It was Bloomer's turn to do the report. But if it had been left to him alone, the report would have taken about a month to produce and would still only have been about two sentences long. So Sadiq helped him. And that was the problem. Sadiq was more upset than anyone about the defeat and his version of what happened left no one in any doubt as to who was to blame.

...Bad Boyz were set for a good draw when Jordan made a stupid mistake in the very last minute. Instead of clearing the ball, she stupidly passed it across her own goalmouth to Bloomer. But it didn't get to him. The Hornets striker got the ball and scored an easy goal. Thanks to Jordan, Hornets won.

When Jordan read this, she was furious. She had a scowl on her that could scare the dead.

"You're not putting that up on the notice-board!" she stormed at Bloomer. She took the report to Mr Davies. He called the team together at lunchtime.

"Now, look," he said, "you've got to pull together after a defeat. Blaming one another won't do anyone any good."

"But it *was* her fault," Sadiq grumbled.

For once, Kyle was on his side. "Yeah, Jordan," he agreed, pointing a chunky finger. "You gave the ball straight to that bloke's feet."

43

Jordan's face seethed with outrage. "Well, I didn't mean to did I, you big moron. Bloomer could easily have got the ball, if he'd been paying attention for once."

"I was payin' attention," Bloomer squeaked. "It weren't my fault, it was yours."

"OK, OK!" Mr Davies shouted. "Look, everyone makes mistakes. It's not important. What's important is that you learn from them."

"Yeah, well I have," Jordan muttered grimly. "I've learnt what a lot of wallies you lot are." And with that, she stormed out of the room.

"You shouldn't have called her stupid, Bloomer," Dareth said. "You know what she's like."

"Yeah, stupid," said Sadiq, and he marched out too.

The team was well and truly divided with Sadiq, Kyle and Bloomer on one side and Jordan, supported by Dareth and Max, on the other. Sung-Woo, meanwhile, was busy with his tables.

From being delighted a week before, Mr Davies was a worried man. His team was falling apart and just days before their most important match yet: the top of the table clash with Terminators. The winners would be declared champions for the first half of the season. And that wasn't all. The chairman of the Doorstep Dairy was coming to watch!

Over the next couple of days, Mr Davies tried to get his side to make up. But if anything, the division got worse. On the day before the game Bloomer complained to his coach that Jordan had spray-painted his front wall with graffiti.

"What did she write?" Mr Davies inquired with a heavy heart.

"'Bloomer is a dir,'" said Bloomer.

"I see," said Mr Davies, relieved that it wasn't something worse.

"My mum hasn't seen it yet, but she'll go mad when she does," Bloomer squeaked.

"OK, leave it with me, Bloomer," Mr Davies sighed.

At lunchtime, he confronted Jordan.

"Did you spray graffiti on Bloomer's wall?" he demanded.

"Might have," she shrugged. Her face was

sullen and defiant, the way it used to be most of the time before Bad Boyz existed.

Mr Davies gave her a searching look. "You can't do that kind of thing, Jordan. It's just not acceptable. You know that."

"He started it," she retorted, "calling me stupid."

"Well, two wrongs don't make a right. And spray-painting someone's wall is vandalism. If Mr Fisher found out, you know what he'd do."

She nodded. Once before when she'd graffitied a wall in a fit of anger, he'd managed to save her from being expelled – but it had been a near thing.

"This time you'd be in big trouble, Jordan. Is that what you want?"

She shrugged again.

"Jordan, look at me," Mr Davies pleaded. Her head lifted very slowly. "Don't throw it all away. Please." Jordan said nothing. "I'll get some cleaning stuff from the caretaker and you go round and clean that wall up straight after school. OK?"

"All right," Jordan muttered reluctantly.

"And I'll have a word with the others," said Mr Davies.

But the others were being equally stubborn.

What kind of display would they put on, Mr Davies worried, when they weren't even speaking to each other? The situation looked bleak.

9

It was a perfect morning for football. The sun beamed down warmth and goodwill on the world.

In the Bad Boyz changing room, however, the mood was anything but sunny. One by one, the players arrived with unsmiling faces, looking as if the last thing they wanted to do was play football.

Hardly a word was spoken. Even Max was quiet. They got into their kit, put on their boots and sat in two groups on either side of Sung-Woo.

Bloomer hadn't arrived.

Mr Davies glanced at his watch. There were fifteen minutes to kick-off. They should have been outside warming-up by now.

"Does anyone know where Bloomer is?"

48

he asked.

No one did.

"Has anyone spoken to him this morning?"

No one had.

Mr Davies sighed. Things were going from bad to worse. Bloomer had his faults as a player, but the team was a lot better off with him than without him. Taking the field a player light against your nearest challengers was not a clever ploy; it would be tough enough with seven.

"All right—" he began, wondering what on earth he could say to turn this situation round when the changing room door suddenly opened.

All eyes turned to look at the small figure who stood there. It was Bloomer, and his face glistened with tears.

"Sorry I'm late," he sobbed.

"Bloomer! What's the matter?" Mr Davies called.

Bloomer wiped away a tear from one damp, pink cheek.

"It's, well, me ... me hamster died," he squeaked, then burst into tears.

At once, and as one, his team-mates went to

comfort him. They huddled round him – even Jordan – all enmity put aside in the light of this tragedy. They all had pets that they loved – from grass snakes to Labradors – and immediately sympathized with Bloomer's sadness.

There was a knock at the door.

"Hello!" A man's voice called. "Are you decent? Can we come in?"

"It's my dad," said Max.

The door opened slowly and Max's dad's face appeared.

"Sorry to interrupt your team meeting," he said. "But I've got an important visitor out here who wants to meet you."

"It's the Queen!" Max exclaimed and the others laughed.

"Don't be daft, Max," chided his dad. He stepped into the room, followed by a tall, thick-set man with a ruddy complexion and a wide smile.

"This is Mr Machin, boys, the chairman of the Doorstep Dairy," said Max's dad. He introduced Mr Davies to Mr Machin and they shook hands.

"I'm told you lot are top of the league," said

Mr Machin warmly. "Must be all that milk you drink."

Jordan pulled a face. She hated milk and was just about to say so, when Mr Davies spoke.

"I think we should show Mr Machin our appreciation for sponsoring us. Well, Dareth?"

"Yeah," Dareth agreed. He raised his thumb. "Cheers, mate."

"How about giving Mr Machin three proper cheers?" Mr Davies suggested. "Hip, hip ..."

"...hooray!"

"Hip, hip ..."

"...hooray!"

"Hip, hip ..."

"...hooray!"

Mr Machin looked pleased, but a little embarrassed. "Thanks a lot," he said. "Now, we'll let you get on with your team talk. Best of luck." He nodded at Mr Davies and then he and Max's dad walked to the door. Just as he was about to go out Mr Machin turned and remarked, "You know, you look just like Brazil in those shirts. I hope you play like them. Up the Bad Boyz!"

The roar that met this exclamation almost blew the Doorstep Dairy chairman out of the changing room.

The Bad Boyz were a team again!

10

Terminators kicked off and were the stronger team in the opening minutes. They had a very dangerous player up front, Asif, who was quick and strong and difficult to tackle. Fortunately for Bad Boyz, his early runs were out wide and he had no real support in the middle.

Meanwhile, Bad Boyz were struggling to get into any rhythm. They seemed to be trying too hard – Dareth and Sung-Woo in particular. Every time they got the ball, they ran with it and took on opponents rather than passing. Terminators were very strong in defence, playing with three players at the back, so even if Dareth or Sung-Woo got past a couple of defenders there was always another one there to beat. They just couldn't get past the last man.

Surprisingly, however, it was Bad Boyz who scored first. Sung-Woo ran on to a long clearance by Sadiq and shot early. It wasn't one of his best efforts and the keeper seemed to have it well covered. But somehow he let the ball slip through his legs and into the goal.

"Unlucky, son!" called Mr Machin kindly. "Keep your head up!"

"And your legs together!" added Max's dad quietly.

To their credit, Terminators continued to take the game to Bad Boyz – and still looked the more dangerous team. Asif hit the post and then shot straight at Kyle when clean through on goal.

"Great save, Kyle!" shouted Mr Davies as the keeper booted the ball clear. Kyle gave his manager a huge gloopy grin.

It was only a matter of time before Terminators equalized; they were having all the play. Near the end of the first half, Asif took the ball past Jordan and then dummied to go outside Max, cutting into the penalty area instead. Wrong-footed, Max tripped him up. It was a clear penalty – well, clear that is, to everyone except Sadiq!

"Oh, ref!" he complained.

Asif took the kick himself and scored. Kyle got a hand to the shot but it was too powerful and he couldn't keep it out.

"Good effort, son!" Mr Machin called. He was really into this match – as were all the spectators. It really was gripping stuff.

At last the whistle went for half-time. While the players sucked their oranges, Mr Davies gave them a pep talk.

"Let's get our passing game going," he said. "Dareth, Sung-Woo, heads up when you've got the ball. Assess your options. Look for the player in space." He told Jordan and Bloomer to push forward a bit to put more pressure on the Terminators' defence. The instruction to Max and Sadiq was to try to keep Asif out wide and not let him run in on goal. "Then, if you do foul him, it won't matter too much."

Max put his fingers to his mouth and grimaced. "Sorry about the penalty," he said.

"Don't worry about it," said Mr Davies. "Just don't do it again."

As they prepared to line up for the second half, Mr Davies had a quiet word with Bloomer. "How are you feeling?" he asked.

"Are you coping all right?"

"Yeah," Bloomer replied with a puzzled look, as if he couldn't understand the question. It was almost as if he'd forgotten all about his hamster!

Bad Boyz started the second half much better. They were passing the ball and causing Terminators more problems. They made a number of good chances in the first five minutes, but missed them all – Sung-Woo being the main culprit. They looked like being costly misses too, because soon after, the Terminators goalie booted the ball clear and Asif sprinted past both Max and Sadiq, dribbled round Kyle and shot into an empty net. Were Terminators going to snatch the title from Bad Boyz right at the death?

"Come on, Bad Boyz!" Mr Davies urged.

"Show them what you're made of, Bad Boyz!" cried Mr Machin. He was truly into the match!

"This is very exciting, isn't it?" he said to Max's dad with a smile.

"Too exciting," said Max's dad with a shake of his head.

Bad Boyz responded well. They started to

put together some really good moves. Jordan and Bloomer pushed forward and made some excellent runs down the flanks. At last, Bad Boyz were stretching the Terminators back line.

Chances came – and went. On another day, Sung-Woo might have had a hat-trick in the second half alone. He hit the post, shot narrowly wide and missed his kick entirely right in front of the goal. Dareth had a fine shot saved and Jordan saw an effort cleared off the line. It started to look as if Bad Boyz would never score. Then, midway through the second half, Dareth was brought down in the penalty area.

"Penalty!" the Bad Boyz spectators cried as one.

The referee pointed to the spot. Dareth placed the ball and walked back. Mr Davies could hardly bear to watch.

The referee blew his whistle. Dareth trotted forward and kicked the ball. He didn't hit it cleanly, but the ball rolled towards the corner of the net. The goalie was well beaten. It looked like a certain goal – but no! The ball bounced against the post and straight into the goalie's arms. Dareth put his head in his hands. He couldn't believe it – and neither could the spectators!

"I don't think I could take this every week," sighed Mr Machin.

"No," Max's dad agreed.

Mr Davies was speechless. It seemed like it just wasn't going to be Bad Boyz' day.

Moments later, Terminators almost increased their lead. Asif fired in a scorching volley that appeared destined for the top corner – but somehow, Kyle got one of his giant hands to it and pushed the ball away for a corner. Then he bawled at his defenders for not covering properly.

Bad Boyz attacked again and again, but still Terminators held firm. There were just five minutes left – and still no breakthrough. It looked as if Bad Boyz would have to settle for being runners-up.

With three minutes left, Max decided to go on the charge. He went through two tackles and carried on running. There were four Bad Boyz players ahead of him now and only three Terminators defenders back.

"Pass it, Max!" shrieked Dareth.

But Max didn't seem to hear. He ran on

towards goal and tried to go past another defender. This time, he was tackled. But the ball fell kindly for Sung-Woo and he shot first time. He scuffed his shot rather and the keeper got a hand to the ball, parrying it to one side … right into the path of Bloomer! Time seemed to stand still as Bloomer moved forward, lifted his left foot and kicked the ball … straight into the back of the net!

"YES!" Bad Boyz had equalized! It was 2–2. The players went wild. They chased Bloomer and leapt on him. Max knelt on the ground and beat his chest with his fists. Kyle lay on his back in the goalmouth. Then the others did a bizarre kind of dance, pretending to be chickens.

As it happened, there was soon further cause for celebration. A minute later, Bad Boyz scored again to secure victory with an excellent team move, in which every player was involved. Kyle threw the ball to Sadiq, who passed to Max. He knocked the ball to Jordan, who flicked the ball first time to Dareth. He went past one opponent before sliding the ball out to Bloomer on the left wing. A quick sprint and cross and the ball was at the feet of Sung-Woo, running in on goal. Without breaking stride, the striker lashed the ball high into the net. And that was it! Bad Boyz had won the game and were champions of the first half of the Appleton Little League!

"Congratulations! That last goal was a beauty," cooed Mr Machin, shaking Mr Davies' hand. His ruddy face beamed with pleasure. "Just like Brazil, in fact..."

11 ⚽

"Champions, champions!"

It was the Monday lunchtime after the match with Terminators, and Bad Boyz were celebrating all over again. Only Sadiq wasn't looking totally happy.

"I still say that wasn't a penalty," he grumbled.

"Course it was," Max disagreed. "If I was doing a match report, I'd say I hacked that boy down like … like a knife through butter."

"That's good. I like that," said Kyle. "It's like my brilliant save at the end. You could say I flew through the air like … like…"

"Like a flabby bag of sick," Jordan suggested and the others laughed.

"Oi, watch it!" Kyle exclaimed, his podgy face scowling.

Jordan mimed innocence. "I never did nuffing," she said and the others laughed again. This time even Kyle grinned.

"Well," Dareth declared emphatically, "it doesn't matter how you say it – we're the CHAMPIONS!"

There was a great roar of approval.

Teams	Played	Wo
Bad Boyz	7	6
Hornets	7	4
Terminators	7	4
Dorking Runners	7	3
Vinnie's Vulcans	7	3
Eddy's Eagles	7	1
X Club 7	7	0
Dart United	7	0

"And Sung-Woo's got the final table to prove it," said Mr Davies. "Isn't that right, Sung-Woo?"

Sung-Woo nodded. "I made copies for everyone," he said, passing them round.

The final table looked like this:

Drawn	Lost	For	Against	Points
0	1	29	11	18
3	0	22	8	15
1	2	25	9	13
3	1	16	14	12
1	3	19	12	10
3	3	15	17	6
2	5	5	25	2
1	6	3	38	1

"That's excellent, Sung-Woo," Mr Davies said. "Well done. Well done all of you." He gave his team an appreciative smile. "And a special well done to Bloomer." Bloomer's cheeks whooshed red. "For showing such courage in the face of adversity. We all know how upsetting it is to lose a pet."

There was a mumble of agreement from all – except Sung-Woo. He frowned and shook his head. "Bloomer no *lose* his pet," he insisted. "His hamster dead."

Mr Davies sighed.

"It's all right," said Bloomer, "I got another pet now."

"Another hamster?" Mr Davies asked.

"No, I got a rat."

"One of those white ones?" said Jordan. "My cousin had one of them. They're really clever. They can do tricks and stuff."

Bloomer shook his head. "Nah, it ain't white," he said. "It's sort of dirty brown. I caught it round me dustbin the other night."

"And has your pet got a name?" Mr Davies inquired.

"Yeah, course it has," squeaked Bloomer. "I called him Bad Boy."

There was another approving cheer.

"He could be our mascot," said Dareth brightly.

"Oh, that's all I need," said Mr Davies, "a wild rat rampaging about the changing room." He picked up his copy of the final league table and waved it at his grinning players. "I think your matches are quite exciting enough, don't you?"

The complete results of the first half of the Appleton Little League

Week 1

Bad Boyz (4)	vs	Vinnie's Vulcans (2)
Terminators (2)	vs	Hornets (2)
Dorking Runners (3)	vs	X Club 7 (1)
Dart United (0)	vs	Eddy's Eagles (4)

Week 2

Bad Boyz (5)	vs	Dorking Runners (2)
Vinnie's Vulcans (6)	vs	X Club 7 (0)
Hornets (1)	vs	Eddy's Eagles (1)
Terminators (9)	vs	Dart United (0)

Week 3

Bad Boyz (7)	vs	Dart United (0)
Vinnie's Vulcans (3)	vs	Eddy's Eagles (2)
Dorking Runners (2)	vs	Terminators (1)
Hornets (4)	vs	X Club 7 (1)

Week 4

Bad Boyz (5)	vs	Eddy's Eagles (3)
Vinnie's Vulcans (6)	vs	Dart United (1)
Hornets (3)	vs	Dorking Runners (3)
Terminators (5)	vs	X Club 7 (0)

Week 5
Bad Boyz (4)	vs	X Club 7 (0)
Hornets (8)	vs	Dart United (0)
Vinnie's Vulcans (1)	vs	Dorking Runners (1)
Terminators (4)	vs	Eddy's Eagles (1)

Week 6
Bad Boyz (1)	vs	Hornets (2)
Terminators (2)	vs	Vinnie's Vulcans (1)
Dorking Runners (2)	vs	Eddy's Eagles (2)
X Club 7 (1)	vs	Dart United (1)

Week 7
Bad Boyz (3)	vs	Terminators (2)
X Club 7 (2)	vs	Eddy's Eagles (2)
Hornets (2)	vs	Vinnie's Vulcans (0)
Dorking Runners (3)	vs	Dart United (1)

Follow Bad Boyz on their Little League cup run in the third book of this series.

K.O. KINGS

Coming soon!

(Turn the page to read the first chapter.)

1

"Catch it, Kyle, you big blob!"

The Bad Boyz keeper turned and glared at the shouting figure on the touchline. He'd just turned a fierce shot round the post and he reckoned it had been a pretty good save.

"Don't take any notice," said Jordan. She clapped a hand on Kyle's broad shoulder. "That was wicked."

"Who is that geezer anyway?" growled Sadiq, waving a clenched fist towards the touchline.

"Yeah, who's he calling a big blob?" said Max. "Great ugly gorilla." He put his hands in his armpits, pulled a face and started making gorilla noises. Next to him, Bloomer squeaked with laughter and joined in. They were still monkeying around when the corner came over. Luckily, Dareth, the captain, was paying attention to the game and booted the ball clear.

"Come on, Bad Boyz! Concentrate!" called Mr Davies. He was both the Bad Boyz manager and their teacher at school. He glanced along the touchline. He was used to being his team's only supporter and he wondered who the man was who'd shouted at Kyle.

Mr Davies had never seen him before, but he was obviously someone who knew Kyle well. All his comments had been directed at the keeper – and none had been complimentary. Luckily, Kyle was in a pretty good mood. The match was almost over and he hadn't let in a goal. At the other end, Bad Boyz had struck three times and were well set for a comfortable win.

It was the first round of the Appleton Little League Cup. Bad Boyz' opponents were X Club 7. In his pre-match team talk, Mr Davies had called them "the most improved team in the league".

"Yeah," Dareth had agreed. "But they're still pants."

They'd looked anything but pants in the first

half, though. The game had been very even and Kyle had had to make a number of fine saves – though none of them good enough for the man on the touchline. When Kyle parried the ball, he should have caught it; when he saved with his feet, he should have used his hands; when he booted the ball clear, he should have picked it up...

At half-time only one goal had separated the teams – and that had been a fluke. A corner from Jordan had rebounded off the post, hit a defender on the heel and bounced back over the line.

In the second half, though, Bad Boyz had been well on top. Sung-Woo, their main striker, had scored twice and could have had three or four more. Jordan had hit the post with a scorching shot and Dareth had had a header cleared off the line.

To their credit, X Club 7 carried on battling to the end, even though they were obviously very tired. It was due to this tiredness that they gave away a penalty in the last minute. A weary defender stumbled and tripped Sung-Woo as the striker chased a long kick from Kyle. It was a clear penalty.

Dareth offered the ball to Sung-Woo. "You take it," he said. "Get your hat-trick."

But Sung-Woo shook his head with a characteristic frown. "You the penalty taker," he insisted. "I have two goals already. You score."

Dareth shrugged. "All right. Cheers," he said.

He placed the ball on the spot and took a couple of steps backwards. Then he trotted forward and blasted the ball into the top right-hand corner of the net. At once he wheeled round and began his latest celebration. This involved cupping one hand round his ear and flapping the other like a wing. He was well into his celebration before he noticed that no one else was joining in. They were all just standing looking at him.

Dareth's hands dropped and so did his smile. "Wasup?" he said, puzzled.

Jordan nodded towards the goal. "Look," she said.

Dareth turned. The referee was still standing by the penalty spot with his arms folded. "Take it again," he ordered. "And this time, wait till I blow my whistle."

"I thought you did blow," said Dareth.

The referee shook his head.

Dareth grinned. "Must have been Bloomer then," he said.

Once more he placed the ball on the penalty spot.

Once more he took a couple of steps back.

He waited.

The referee blew his whistle.

Once more, Dareth ran forward and blasted the ball ... but this time into the top left-hand corner.

He raised his hands and started to turn, but before he could, Bloomer and Max had jumped him. A moment later, Kyle tumbled on top and all four fell in a screeching heap.

The mystery man on the touchline was not amused. "Get back in goal, Kyle, you idiot!" he barked. "The game's not over!" But he was wrong. For at that instant the referee blew the final whistle.

Bad Boyz had beaten X Club 7 by 4–0, the same score as in the league.

They were through to the next round of the cup!

Author's Note

Although Appleton Little League is my own creation, it's based on an organization that really exists. Little League Football is a registered charity that provides free football for children from eight to thirteen years old in over thirty leagues around the country. The emphasis is on enthusiasm and effort rather than ability – players are encouraged to develop team spirit, self-discipline and sportsmanship. It's also a lot of fun and a good place to start playing organized football. Players join individually rather than as a team, as in my series, but most of the rules are as I've described them. If you want to find out more, check out the Little League Football website:

www.littleleaguefootball.com

There may be a league on your doorstep!

If you're interested in joining a Sunday junior football team, a useful site to look at is:

www.juniorleague.net

It has details of teams and leagues right across the country.

If you like playing football, there's a team out there for you!

To ask Alan Durant anything about the Bad Boyz series – or any football matter – you can contact him by e-mail at:

alan.durant@walker.co.uk

He'd love to hear from you!